Mark O'Neill has been writing for many years and enjoys writing various genres. He writes mainly for himself and stories that he would like to read or see, whether it be a book, play or movie. His writing technique involves working on three stories at once. That way, he says, if he hits a block on one story (or gets bored), he can move to another. Mark's idea is to write things he himself enjoys reading and doesn't stick to any type of story.

For Keri and Michael, my children whom I adore beyond reason. This is for you.

Mark O'Neill

God – A Christmas
Visit

AUSTIN MACAULEY PUBLISHERS™

LONDON • CAMBRIDGE • NEW YORK • SHARJAH

A CIP catalogue record for this title is available from the British Library.

ISBN 9781528941839 (Paperback)
ISBN 9781528970891 (ePub e-book)

www.austinmacauley.com

First Published (2020)
Austin Macauley Publishers Ltd
25 Canada Square
Canary Wharf
London
E14 5LQ

Thanks to everyone who believed in me and to those who didn't. You all made me want to succeed. To Mhairi who nagged me constantly to write this story, it's finally done. Now please give me peace.

Scene 1

It is the week before Christmas, Oxford Street, London.

A woman called Mary is in a store buying some Christmas presents for the staff in her office. She is a Junior Manager. Mary no longer loves Christmas and is buying very non-personal gifts, she has a basket full of notebooks, pens, staplers etc. and looks harassed.

She takes the basket to the counter. The shop assistant takes the basket and looks at it.

Shop Assistant: "Running out of supplies in the office madam?"

Mary: "No, last minute Christmas shopping."

Shop Assistant: "Erm…I'm sorry. CHRISTMAS shopping???"

Mary: "Yes. Could you add up please? I need to get these back to the office to wrap them for the staff."

Shop Assistant: "Are they all on Santa's naughty list?"

Mary: "Excuse me?"

Shop Assistant: "Or perhaps some paper clips to add a bit of glitter and excitement?"

Mary: "Funny! Just fill them please."

Shop Assistant: "Certainly madam. Would you like me to individually wrap the staples?"

Scene 2

Outside the shop, on the other side of the street a man appears.

It is God in human form, he is staring at the shop Mary is in and then starts walking down Oxford Street.

He stops at a Salvation Army band, where a small crowd has formed. The band is about to strike up.

Band Leader: "Okay, let's try again and hope we get it right… God willing."

God: "I'll try my best."

The band starts. They are terrible. The crowd winces and sniggers. The band stops.

The band leader speaks to the person behind him, God.

BL: "We're not very good I'm afraid, we try our best but most of us can't really play."

God: "Oh, I don't know. I think you just need a little bit of faith."

BL: "Thanks, but even the Almighty couldn't get a tune out of this lot."

God: "You reckon? Tell you what, give it another go. (Pauses) How about Good King Wenceslas? That was always my favourite, he was a nice man too."

BL: "Erm…okay. But cover your ears."

God: (leaning to the bandleader and whispers) "Have faith…"

The band starts to play, their notes are perfect, and they sound like an orchestra. The Band leader is staggered and delighted.

God starts singing and the crowd joins in.

God smiles.

Across the street, a woman who has an overload of presents, loses control of her pram and baby, and it falls onto the busy road with a car zooming towards it.

Woman: "Oh my God, someone please help!"

God sees this and with the lift of one finger the cars tyres burst, and it stops dead. The driver jumps out.

God stops the pram and gives it back to the grateful mother.

God: "Merry Christmas, here is your child my dear (Pauses) and I think this may be of help."

God produces a large shopping bag and puts the presents in and hands it to the woman.

Woman: (teary and hysterical) "Thank you so much."

God: "Take care of him now, he'll score the winner in the cup final one day."

God stops a taxi and puts the woman and baby in.

The driver of the car is on the mobile to the breakdown services.

God: "Why are you calling breakdown assistance?"

Driver: "You nuts mate, look at me tyres!"

The driver looks at his tyres, they are perfect.

Driver: "But…but…what the f…"

God puts his finger on the driver's lips.

God: "No swearing now…it's Christmas."

God just smiles and walks on. Driver scratches his head.

Mary is rushing from the shop as she is running late and runs straight into God, they both fall to the ground the gifts scatter everywhere.

Mary: "Oh, I'm so sorry. Are you okay?"

God: "I'm fine. Thank you."

Mary: "I'm sorry. I just wasn't looking, I'm in such a rush… Oh, my gifts…"

God: "Please let me help you." (extends his hand) "My name is George. George O'Donnell."

God picks up gifts.

God: "Are these presents?"

Mary: "I'm Mary. Oh…he…yes, for my staff. I work in an office."

God: "Not very Christmassy."

Mary: "Neither am I. Thank you for your help."

God: "Not at all, please let me help you carry these to your office."

Mary: "No it's fine, thank you."

God: "Honest, it's not a problem."

God smiles and Mary smiles back.

Mary: "Oh okay, thank you."

They start walking down the street and are chatting.

Mary: "So, are you from London?"

God: "Oh no, I'm just visiting. Doing tourist stuff, I like to see the Christmas lights."

Mary: "Oh right, okay."

God: "So, do you really not like Christmas?"

Mary: (not answering) "So, are you here in London long?"

God: "Oh not long, just long enough to see a few sights and soak up the Christmas atmosphere. So, Mary why do you dislike Christmas?"

Mary: "Well, here we are at my office. Listen, thank you so much...erm..."

God: "George."

Mary: "Yes, eh George, thank you so much for your kindness. If there's anything I can do to repay you."

God: "This is where you work?"

Mary: "Yep, this is me, listen I'm really late for a meeting so..."

God: "No, sorry, not at all. Listen, if you're free, perhaps we could go for a coffee or something."

Mary: "Oh, that's sweet but I don't really think so..."

God: "You did say, if you could repay me...and a promise is a promise..."

Mary: (in a rush) "Okay... erm, tomorrow about 1.00 at the café on the corner."

God: "Great, see you then."

Mary rushes upstairs to the office.

Scene 3

Mary rushes into the manager's office.

Mary: "Mr Thomas, I'm so sorry I'm late. I was trying to get the gifts for the staff, and I bumped into this man and…"

Mr Thomas: "Mary what are you talking about? You only left about 10 minutes ago. You must be a fast shopper."

Mary: "What, no, I've been away ages…I don't…erm…"

Mary checks her watch. It has only been 10 minutes

Mr Thomas: "Think you're working too hard, Mary." (Laughs)

Mary closes manager's door behind her totally bemused.

God is standing outside and smirks, knowingly.

Scene 4

On the office floor. A young man, Peter, is carrying some files, he is awkward and geek type. He is trying to talk to a girl, Maggie, who he fancies. She is very pretty and is the office pin up.

Peter: (Nervously) "Hello Maggie."

Maggie: "Hi Peter, how are you?"

Peter: "I'm very well…erm…I have those copies you asked for…erm…"

Maggie: "Thanks Peter."

Peter: "You can call me Pete…if you want…"

Maggie: "Okay…Pete."

Peter: (boyish snigger) "Can I call you Margaret?"

Maggie: "No…Maggie is fine."

Peter: "Oh…"

A couple of office jocks appear, Andy and Phil. Full of themselves. They love Maggie but they hate Peter.

Andy: "Hey Petesy…how's the trainspotting going?"

Phil: "Yeah, read any good comic books man?" (laughs)

They knock Peter's photocopying out of his hand.

Maggie: "Guys, give it a rest."

Maggie bends over and helps Peter pick up the files.

Andy and Phil stare at her backside.

Andy: "Wow, I know what I want for Christmas."

Phil: "Yeah in my sack!"

Maggie turns and glares. She speaks to Peter.

Maggie: "You okay?"

Peter: "I'm…I'm fine, thanks."

Maggie: "Thanks for copying these for me Peter…Pete."

Peter smiles and walks away.

Maggie: "Why don't you two grow up and stop picking on him. Oh, by the way, Phil... (moves in close to him) ...your tie is in my coffee."

The whole office laughs at Phil who rushes away embarrassed.

Scene 5

Lunchtime, the same day. Mary is out for a coffee. She is quite stressed as she has an important work presentation to do and it may get her the promotion she desperately wants, behind her in the next table is God, who turns around.

God: "Mary! Hello fancy meeting you here."

Mary: "Hi…erm George. (Half serious) Are you following me?"

God: "Oh Mary, not at all, we did have a date at 1.00 today, can I join you?" (He moves to her table)

Mary: "Actually George, I'm rather busy now, if you don't…"

God: "Great, thanks (He sits down). So, what you doing?"

Mary: (sighs) "I'm trying to get this work presentation right."

God: "Oh…important stuff eh?"

Mary: "Very!"

God: "Can I help?"

Mary: "Not unless you are good at getting important messages across to a tough audience." (laughs)

God: "Well, the Egyptians were hard to convince but that Red Sea thing was a belter."

Mary: (not listening) "Sorry, what?"

God: "Never mind, coffee?"

Mary: "Erm …yes thanks."

God: (to waitress) "Hi, can we have one light Americana." (Mary's favourite)

Mary: "How did you know that was my favourite?"

God: "Divine intervention, oh and can I have a large café latte with extra cream, sprinkles, marshmallows, nuts and chocolate sauce please? Oh, and three muffins please…chocolate chip."

Mary stares at him.

Mary: "Wow, you have a sweet tooth."

God: "You know…I don't know if I have. I've never tried before."

Mary: (Laughs) "You know George…you're weird."

God: "I don't think I've been called that before."

Mary: "Really? I'm amazed. George…who are you?"

God: "Told you, just visiting, I like to take the Christmas experience in."

Mary: "Don't they have Christmas where you're from then?"

God: "Oh yeah, it's big where I am…but nice to experience it down here."

Mary: "Down here? Oh, you're from up North."

God: "Oh yes…very North."

Waitress: "Hi. Here is your light Americana madam."

Mary: "Thank you."

Waitress: "And here is your large café latte with extra cream, sprinkles, marshmallows, nuts and chocolate sauce."

God: "Mmm…"

Waitress: "And three chocolate chip muffins!"

God: "Wow…this looks amazing."

Mary: "So, George."

God starts spooning his drink into his mouth. He is delirious with the new taste sensations.

Mary: "Where is it you are from?"

God: "Aww (drinking the latte and eating the muffins) Heaven, and I should know! This is incredible. No wonder you guys love this so much. I mean it's just a cocoa bean and you made it into this. That's amazing! I never thought of that."

Mary laughs as God's face is covered in the food.

Mary: "Don't they have chocolate muffins where you are George?"

God: (Slurping) "Nope, they don't exist where I am, don't need them."

God calls the waitress over.

God: "Please can I have another?"

Mary: "Don't you worry about putting on weight?"

God: "No…I've been the same weight, like, forever."

Mary looks at God and is captured by his almost childlike innocence and charisma. Who is this strange man?

The scene then shifts to the end as they go to pay.

Mary: "Here, let me."

God: "I'm sorry, of course money, I don't have any."

Mary: "Hmmmm. My treat, don't you have a job."

God: "Oh yes, an important one, but I don't get paid."

Mary: "Oh, volunteer work?"

God: "Oh, very much so."

Mary: "Like a social worker."

God: "Erm… kind of, yes. Very rewarding."

Scene 6

Mary and God are walking towards Mary's office. Chatting.

Mary: "Well, thank you for the company it was…interesting."

God: "You're welcome, I loved it."

Mary: (Wiping some chocolate sauce from his face) "Yes, I can see that."

God: "Mary. I'm actually looking for a place to stay while I'm in London, somewhere to rent. Do you know of anywhere?"

Mary: "Well, I'm renting out my top floor room in my house, but I'd prefer you went through my letting agency."

God: "Oh please, it would only be a few days."

Mary: "You don't have a job, George."

God: "Leave that with me, please?"

Mary: "I don't know. I'd rather…"

God: (In a childlike pathetic way, fluttering his eyelids) "Pleeeeeease?"

Mary: (laughs). "Okay, but only if you get a job and can pay me."

God: "Great. It's a deal then."

Mary: "Okay. I just hope I can trust you."

God: "Believe me, I'm the one person on the whole planet you CAN trust."

Mary: "Okay, well here's the address. When you get a job let me know."

God: "Thanks Mary, you won't regret it."

Mary: "I hope not." (walks away)

Scene 7

Mary is in the office frantically worrying about this presentation she is going to give at the Boardroom meeting in a few days. A colleague, Judith, comes to talk to her.

Judith: "Hi Mary. You okay? You look a bit stressed."

Mary: "Hi Judith. Sorry, yeah, I am a bit…"

Judith: "What's up? (Tries to peer at Mary's laptop.). What you working on?"

Mary: (Hiding it) "Oh nothing, just something I've been trying to do for a few weeks."

Judith: "Anything I can help with. I mean we're friends eh?"

Mary: "Yeah well okay, I'm working on a presentation for the next board meeting and I'm not sure if I've got it right. I've gone over and over it, and every time I do, it seems worse."

Judith: "Look, why don't you email me a copy and I'll go over it and see how it reads. If there's anything I think is not right, I'll not send it back."

Mary: "Oh Judith, would you? That would be a real help."

Judith: "Of course, now why don't you head off home and see that lovely daughter of yours."

Mary: "Thanks Judith, I REALLY appreciate it."

Judith: "Don't mention it. What are friends for?"

Scene 8

Mary arrives home, her 10-year-old daughter, Gabrielle, is there with the child minder.

Gabrielle: "Mummy!" (runs to Mary)

Mary: (Holding Gabrielle) "Hi gorgeous, how's my girl?"

Child minder: "Homework all done."

Mary: "Thanks."

Gabrielle: "Mummy, will you come to the school pantomime?"

Mary: "Sweetheart, Mummy is really busy. I've told you, I may not."

Gabrielle: "Mummy, please!"

Mary: "Baby, I—"

Gabrielle: "Mummy…!"

Mary: "Okay, okay. I'll do what I can do."

Gabrielle: "Thank you, Mummy, you're the best mummy ever."

Scene 9

The next day in work. Mary is at her desk. God is there. He is now working as the mail delivery boy.

God: "Mail for you, Mary."

Mary: (not looking up) "Thanks."

God: "And, how are you today?"

Mary: (looks up) "Oh God!"

God: "Yep, that's right."

Mary: "How did you get in here?"

God: "I work here now, temporary, till end of Christmas."

Mary: "What? Where's David, the normal delivery boy?"

God: "Funny thing, he won a once in a lifetime holiday to the Bahamas. Left this morning, amazing eh? What are the chances? So, I'm filling in till he gets back."

Mary: "That's…a miracle."

God: "They do happen, so I guess now that I have a job?"

Mary: "Yes?"

God: (Raises eyebrows) "Erm…job…room?"

Mary: "Oh God, yes, oh right."

God: "Oh God indeed, yes."

Mary: "Okay well, erm, after work, is that okay?"

God: "Fantastic."

God walks away, cheery and whistling. Mary is stunned.

Scene 10

In the office kitchen Peter is making a tea. God comes in and stands near him. Maggie is also in the kitchen.

God: (to Pete) "Hi."

Peter: "Oh, hello."

God: "You're Peter."

Peter: "Yes, have you just started?"

God: "Yes, today. I'm George." (Extends hand)

Peter: "Nice to meet you."

God: "And you."

Peter: "So, you like it then."

God: "Yeah it's great."

(Puts chocolate sprinkles on his tea)

Peter: "Erm…you like chocolate?"

God: "Oh YEAH…love it…one of my favourite things in creation…it used to be rainbows, but this is brilliant!"

Peter: (laughs)

God: "So… (looking at Maggie) …you like that girl?"

Peter: (Embarrassed) "Oh no, no, no…no not at all."

God: "Oh yeah… (knowingly)…you do though."

Peter: (Nods his head a wee bit…whispers) "Yeah."

God: "Well, go talk to her!"

Peter: "Oh, I couldn't."

God: "Go on…"

Just then, Andy and Phil walk in, they go towards Maggie.

Andy: "Hey Maggie. You gonna get all dolled up for the Christmas party."

Phil: "Maybe we could have a slow dance."

Maggie: "A slow death more like."

Andy: "Aww that's not nice…c'mon. I have some mistletoe here."

Phil: "Where would you like him to put it?"

Maggie: "Why don't you stick it up your—"

God walks in between them…

God: "Sorry. Just getting some milk."

Andy: "Hey, watch it!"

God: "I'm sorry."

Maggie: "Will you leave it? He's just the new guy."

Phil: "Just watch it, pal."

God: "Or what?"

Andy: "Oooooh big man, eh?"

God: "You know, you two have a lot of hot air, you should let that out."

Phil: "Who do you think you're talking…"

Just then Andy and Phil's expression changes. There is then a loud fart, followed by another then another, then another, they both run out farting as they do. The people in the kitchen laugh.

God turns to Peter.

God: "That's your cue."

Peter: "What…oh no."

He shoves him towards Maggie.

Maggie: "Hi Pete."

Peter: "Oh...Hi…erm…Maggie."

Maggie: "Any hot water left?"

Peter: "Yes…it's just off the boil."

Maggie: (stirring tea) "So, you going to the office party?"

Peter: "Oh no…I don't think so."

Maggie: "You should. It'll be a good laugh."

Peter: "No, it's not really my thing."

Maggie: "Oh, and what do you have to do that's better than a party then?"

Peter: "I erm…like movies, DVDs and stuff."

Maggie: "Me too, what sort of films do you like?"

Peter: "Well, I kind of like action films, you know 1980 types."

Maggie: "Really?"

Peter: "Yeah. I know you wouldn't think to look at me."

Maggie: "No, it's not that…I like them too."

Peter: (surprised) "Really?"

Maggie: "Yeah…Stallone."

Peter: "Willis."

Maggie: "Van Damme."

Peter: "Schwarzenegger."

Both Steven Segal!

Maggie: "I Love Steven Segal."

Peter: "Really? He's my favourite of all of them."

Maggie: "Mine too! Wow that's amazing…we should watch some Segal DVDs sometime."

Pete says nothing. He's stunned. God elbows him in the back.

Peter: "Yes, that would be great."

Maggie: "Great. Well, need to go back to work. See ya, Pete."

Peter: "See ya, Maggie."

God: "See, told you."

Peter: "It's a miracle."

God: "Well, it's not up there with the creation of the Earth…but it's close."

Scene 11

God and Mary are heading towards Mary's house with the room for rent.

Mary: "Now, the room isn't much."

God: "Oh, that's fine, I don't do extravagant."

Mary: "Now, the rent is normal price for the area, it includes…"

Suddenly a mugger appears with a gun.

Mugger: "Hey, get in here or I'll shoot."

Mary screams.

God: "Now look, I suggest you put that down."

Mugger: "Shut it skinny or I'll bring you closer to your maker."

God: "Erm…I'm pretty close just now actually, (pauses) but look Zak this is not. This isn't the way to solve your gambling problems."

Mugger: "How did you know my name?"

Mary: "How did you know his name?"

Mugger: "How do you know about my gambling problems?"

Mary: "How DID you know about his gambling problems?"

Mugger: (to Mary) "Stop repeating what I say?"

Mary: "I'll stop repeating what you say."

God: "This is not the answer, put the gun down." (Walks towards mugger)

Mugger: "You a cop! is that it!"

Mary: "George, stop, he'll shoot!"

Mugger: "I mean it, back off! I'll shoot!"

God: "You don't want to do this."

Mugger pulls trigger but nothing happens. God puts his finger on the muggers' forehead.

God: "Zak, if you continue on this path, there will be only one conclusion."

Suddenly there are images flashing through the mugger's mind.

Images of more muggings, robberies, drugs and then final images of him lying in a street, shot and dying. Then there are brief images of hell.

God: "You see? Put that gun down now and change your life. Violence will never solve anything. Never."

The mugger drops the gun and runs. God picks up the gun, crushes it and puts it in nearby skip.

Mary: "That was amazing…"

God: "Thank You."

Mary: "…and bloody stupid! (Grabs God by the lapels) Are you insane? He could've killed you!"

God: "I knew he wouldn't."

Mary: "What. Psychic, are you?"

God: "Erm…sort of."

Mary: "How did you know he would drop the gun?"

God: "Violence. It has never achieved anything; you know every war ends up with both sides sitting around a table talking peace. One day, the human race will learn to do the talking beforehand…it will be so much easier."

They both walk off.

Scene 12

God and Mary arrive at Mary's house. Gabrielle is there with the babysitter.

Mary: "Hi, I'm home."

Gab: "Mummy!"

Mary: "Hey pumpkin."

Gab: "Oh, who's this?"

Mary: "Gabrielle, this is George, Mum's friend from work. He's going to be renting the room upstairs for a few weeks."

God: "Hello Gabrielle (puts out hand). I'm very pleased to meet you."

Mary: "Say hello, Gabrielle."

Gab: "Hello (shakes God's hand). I'm very pleased to meet you too, sir."

God: "Please, call me George."

Mary: "C'mon Gabby, time to get ready for bed. George, I'll show you your room shortly."

God: "No problem, take your time, lovely house."

Mary: "Thanks."

Scene 13

Mary is putting Gabby to bed.

Gab: "Mummy, who is that man?"

Mary: "Told you pumpkin, he's just a friend from Mummy's work, and he needed a place to stay…and we could do with the extra cash for Christmas, eh?"

Gab: "I like him."

Mary: "Really? Why do you say that? You've only just met him."

Gab: "I know, Mummy, but he seems…nice."

Mary: "He is…a bit strange…but nice."

Gab: "Mummy, do you fancy him?"

Mary: "Goodnight Gabby." (Kisses her forehead)

Gab: (Sniggers) "Mummy's got a boyfriend; Mummy's got a boyfriend."

Mary: "Goodnight Gabby." (Switches off bedroom light).

Scene 14

God and babysitter are downstairs. Babysitter is in the kitchen; God is in living room.

Babysitter: "So, have you known Mary long?"

God: "Oh, a long time,"

Babysitter: (not listening) "Oh, that's nice."

Babysitter opens up a tin that has money in it. She takes out some notes.

God appears behind her.

God: "Is that how you repay kindness? By stealing?"

Babysitter: (Shocked) "I…I don't know what you mean."

God: "Put it back."

Babysitter: (Bursts into tears) "Please, please don't tell her, I'm desperate."

God: "You have a good heart and you are betraying yourself. Stealing is not the way for you. You have great things ahead of you."

Babysitter: "You don't even know me, what do you care?"

God: "I care, believe me. You're studying to be a nurse, aren't you?"

Babysitter: "How did you know?" (Sobbing)

God: "One day, you will save many lives, and everyone will know your name."

Great days are to come. Don't deny them with this. (Takes money out of her hand)

Babysitter is crying uncontrollably.

God: "Here (hands her a tissue). No need for tears. (Holds her). I promise I won't tell if you don't steal again."

Babysitter: "I promise…I promise I won't steal again."

God: "I know you won't."

Babysitter walks out of the door and turns.

Babysitter: "Thank you."

God: "No…thank yourself."

Mary comes downstairs.

Mary: "Oh, has the babysitter gone?"

God: "Yeah, she had to steal herself away."

Mary: "Oh, okay. I had a little Christmas bonus for her."

God: "She's had it."

Mary: "Erm…okay…let's show you the room."

Walking up stairs to the room, Mary opens door.

Mary: "Okay, here it is. Sorry it's not much."

God: "Mary, it's perfect."

Mary: "Rent includes food…you don't look like you eat much." (Small laugh)

God: "Honestly it's perfect, just perfect."

Mary: "George?"

God: "Yes?"

Mary: "Where's all your stuff?"

God: "Oh, it's in my old place. I'll get it later."

Scene 15

God and Mary are in the kitchen.

God: "Gabby is a lovely girl."

Mary: "Yes, yes she is."

God: "Mary, where is Gabby's father?"

Mary begins to tear up.

God: "Sorry, I don't mean to pry."

Mary: "No, it's fine."

God: "Tell me."

Mary: "When Gabby was just a baby, Joe, her father, was coming home late from work. It was Christmas Eve and I had asked him to hurry home as it was snowing heavily. He said he'd be okay, but he just wanted to stop off and pick up a final gift for Gabby. It was a teddy bear with a 'Daddy's Girl' jumper, silly little thing, I suppose. (Eyes begin to moisten) After picking it up, the snow became really heavy. (Starts crying). He was hours late; I knew something had happened. When they took me to identify the body, they gave me the bear, (Sobs) Gabs cuddles into it every night, it's all she has of him, not even a memory. God robbed her of that! Not even one small memory, just a silly bear."

God: "Mary. I'm so sorry."

Mary: (Sniffing) "Now you know why I hate Christmas. It's supposed to be a time of giving and God took away the man I loved and my baby's father. Why should I celebrate? I try my best for her, I mean why should she miss out? But my heart's not in it."

God: "I'm so, so sorry."

Mary: "Why should you be sorry? It's not your fault."

God just looks down.

Scene 16

Mary is in the office. She is behind in her work and is on the phone to the babysitter to stay a bit longer to look after Gabby.

Mary: "Look, I'm really sorry, I promise it'll just be a couple of hours. (Pauses then sensing hesitation) I'll pay you double."

Babysitter: (Voice only on phone) "It's not the money but I have my nursing college course tonight. I really need to do it and I can't be late."

Mary: "Please."

Babysitter: "I'm sorry, Mary, I just can't."

God is walking by with a delivery of mail.

God: "Everything okay?"

Mary: "No…not really."

God: "Can I help?"

Mary: "No, it's okay…"

God hesitates, smiles knowingly and walks away.

Mary: (Desperate) "No wait! Look are you doing anything tonight? I need a big favour."

God: "Sure."

Scene 17

God arrives at Mary's house; the babysitter and Gabby are there.

Babysitter: "Mary called and said you would babysit. Thank you for not telling on me. I'm going to my college course tonight."

God: "That's fantastic."

Babysitter smiles. "Gabby's dinner is in the oven and she is to be in bed by seven thirty."

God: "Okay."

Gabby: "Hello George, Mum says you're looking after me tonight."

God: "That's right Gabby. (Pauses and smiles his big innocent smile at her) If that's okay with you."

Gabby: "That's fine, I'll keep you right and let you know when you're getting it wrong."

God: "Thanks, I'm sure you will."

Scene 18

God is trying to get Gabby's dinner ready while she sets out her plate and cutlery.

Gabby: "Have you ever cooked before?"

God: "Erm…no not really."

Gabby: "Well it's mostly cooked, it just needs heating up."

God: "Yeah…how do you do that?"

Gabby: "I'm really too young to be near a cooker but why not just try the microwave."

God: "Microwave?"

Gabby: "The white object there."

God: "Oh right… (puts in plate of food) …and?"

Gabby: "Oh for goodness sake, let me."

Scene jumps to both having their dinner.

Gabby: "We should say grace."

God: "Yes, we should."

Gabby: "Would you like to say it? Mummy never likes to say it."

God: "Erm…no, you can if that's okay."

Gabby: "Okay then. Dear God, I know you are busy, but I just wanted to say hi and thanks very much for the food we're about to eat. Please look after Mummy again tonight, she tries very hard not to show it, but I know that she is still sad since Daddy went to Heaven. She says that you needed him to help you so I hope he's helping out a lot… Oh, and can you tell him I miss him very much and have his teddy with me every night. (Opens one eye and looks at 'George') Err…and please also look after our new friend, George, he's a bit strange God and needs a lot of looking after, but you know that because he is one of yours. Anyway, lots of love Gabby."

God: "That was lovely Gabby."

Gabby: "Do you think he heard me?"

God: "I know he did."

Gabby: "Do you believe in God, George?"

God: "Yes, very much."

Gabby: "Me too, but I'm not happy that he took my daddy away."

God: "I'm sorry."

Gabby: "But I guess it must have been really important or he wouldn't have done it."

God: "I'm sure he wouldn't have, Gabby, your mum seems pretty sad though."

Gabby: "Yeah. She tries to pretend she's okay, but I know she misses Daddy. I hope God makes her happy again one day."

God: "So do I." (Gabby is playing with her food)

God: "Don't you like sprouts?"

Gabby: "They're yuck!"

God: "No, they're great (takes a mouthful. His face changes. He sticks out his tongue and scrapes them back on his plate, Gabby laughs). They're terrible. What was I thinking with them?"

Gabby: "You're funny George…weird but funny."

God: "Thanks! C'mon let's get something to eat."

Gabby: "Mummy says we've to stay here."

God: "Oh we'll be fine, let's go."

Scene 19

Gabby and God are at the Christmas market enjoying walking around the stalls and shows.

Gabby: "This is great George, Mum's never taken me to this kind of thing."

God: "What, no shows, not even a Fayre? Fayres are great."

Gabby: "No never, this is almost perfect George."

God: "Almost?"

Gabby: "Yeah, I wish it would snow."

God: "Well, you know what, if I can, I'll make it snow."

Gabby: "Promise?"

God: "Promise."

Gabby: (Distracted) "George look!" (Gabby points to a stall with a massive snowman as a prize)

God: "Let's go over." (They walk over to stall)

Stall owner: "On you go sweetheart, knock all the tins over and win the big snowman."

God: "On you go Gabby." (Gabby throws three balls right at the tins but they don't go down)

Gabby: "I'm rubbish at this."

Stall owner: "Bad luck sweetheart."

God: "Have another go."

Gabby: "No, it's fine."

God: "Go on, trust me. You never know, it's Christmas." (God pays for three more balls and hands them to Gabby)

Gabby throws the first directly at the tins – nothing. She throws the next at the tins – nothing.

Gabby: "This is useless."

God: "Gabby, have faith, believe in yourself. You don't know what a little faith and prayer can do."

Gabby throws another, the same as the previous throws, (God smiles and focuses on the ball) suddenly it turns and changes direction then smashes the tins, wrecking the stall, the stall owner is stunned.

God: (Smirking) "I believe this young lady has just won. (Stretches his hand out) Snowman please."

Stall owner: (Handing it over, still stunned) "Err...well done..."

Scene 20

Montage of God and Gabby going around the fayre, includes winning more prizes. Dodgems. God eating loads of sweets and chocolate and candy floss. Scene then ends with them on the big wheel. All set to Wizard's 'I Wish It Could Be Christmas Every Day'.

On the big wheel:

God: "You having a nice time?"

Gabby: "Yes, this is so high. Have you ever been up this high?"

God: "Oh, I've been a lot higher."

Gabby looks a little sad.

God: "What's wrong?"

Gabby: "No snow."

God: "Oh, that's right."

The big wheel stops, and they are both at the top. God releases harness and stands up.

Gabby: "George, we'll fall off!!!"

God: "Don't worry, we're safe."

He looks up, smiles and softly says, "Snow." It begins to snow. He sits back down, pulls down the harness and the wheel begins to move.

God looks at Gabby, who is smiling, "See, a promise is a promise."

Scene 21

Mary comes home, it's quiet, and no one is around. She goes from room to room, shouting, panic increasing by the second as they are not there…

Mary: "Hello? Gabby? (Walks into room) Gabby? (Runs downstairs) Gabby? George! (Gets mobile and dials 999) Hello police, please help, my daughter's gone missing…"

Just then God and Gabby walk in.

Gabby and George: "Hiya, we're home…"

Mary is nearly in tears and immediately shouts at God and Gabby, who both look exhilarated from their trip to the Christmas Fayre. Gabby is clutching the big, toy snowman.

Mary: "Where have you been? (Sobs) You didn't leave a note, I didn't know where you were; I thought something had happened to you!"

Gabby: "Chill Mum, George took me to the Fayre (Excited) and look at all the stuff I won!"

Mary: "Chill! The Fayre? The CHRISTMAS Fayre in town?"

God: "Erm…yeah I took her, I hope that was okay."

Mary tries to compose herself, although she is still seething at God. She hugs Gabby tightly and smiles…

Mary: "Wow, look at all the great things you got! Okay, baby go up and get ready for bed."

Gabby goes upstairs.

(Mary is really angry and turning to God with a sad, scared but furious look on her face).

Mary: "What the hell do you think you were doing?"

God: "What do you mean?"

Mary: "I asked you to babysit. Not KIDNAP her!"

God: "I think you're overreacting."

Mary: "OVERREACTING!!! I come home and find my baby gone, and I'm overreacting! (Pauses to collect her thoughts and inadvertently sobs) And what do you mean taking her to a Christmas Fayre!"

God: "What's wrong with that? She had fun."

Gabby is looking over from the top landing, listening, she is sad and begins to cry. She is holding big white snowman.

Mary: "I don't want her to go to Christmas Fayres."

God: "Why, because you hate Christmas? Why should you deny her the most fabulous of times?"

Mary: "You know why!"

God: "That is not a reason to deny her."

Mary: "How dare you tell me what to do with my daughter? Get out."

God: "Mary…"

Mary: "Get OUT!!!" (She slaps God as the tears stream down her face)

God looks back at her, sad and bemused at the reaction, he leaves. Upstairs Gabby is crying, Mary also starts to cry.

Scene 22

Next morning, Mary and Gabby are having breakfast.

Mary: "You want cornflakes pumpkin?"

Gabby doesn't respond.

Mary: "Orange juice?"

Still no response.

Mary: "Okay. I overreacted; I was just worried. We don't know much about George."

Gabby: "Well, I LIKE him. He's kind and sweet and we had lots of fun."

Mary: "Don't you have fun with me?"

Gabby: "You're always working."

Mary: "Sweetheart it's just…"

Gabby: "Never mind, Mum. (Smiling a sad smile at Mary, Gabby starts pulling things out of the pocket of her house coast) Oh, and here. George wanted you to have this." (Gabby hands Mary an envelope)

Mary: "What's this? (Mary opens envelope. In it is a picture of Gabby with Santa. Mary begins to cry). I'm sorry baby. I'll speak to George today, okay?" (Hugs Gabby)

Gabby: "Okay Mummy."

Scene 23

Mary is back in the office. Staring at the photo. God walks by.

God: "Some mail, Mary."

Mary: "George…look, I'm very sorry. I overreacted, my temper."

God: (smiles) "It's okay. I've destroyed cities with MY temper…"

Mary: "I hope I'm not that bad (laughs). Listen, let me make it up to you; let me cook you dinner. (Hesitates) I'm sure Gabby would love that; she really likes you."

(God smiles his innocent and endearing smile)

God: "Okay, I'll see you tonight."

Mary: "Great and thanks." (Mary bites her lip, has she done the right thing?)

God walks away and Judith walks by.

Mary: "Oh Judith, have you had a chance to look at the presentation?"

Judith: "Oh sorry, not yet. I'll promise I'll look at it today and get back to you."

Mary: "Okay, thanks. I'm going out this afternoon, so I'll catch up with you later."

Judith: "Out?"

Mary: "Yeah, Gabby's panto today."

Judith: "Oh really…well have fun."

Mary: "Okay, thanks."

Scene 24 (No dialogue)

Mary is in the audience of the school panto. Gabby is playing an angel. Mary is smiling as the children sing away in a manger. Her thoughts drift to the past and images of her Husband and tears roll down her face. It's bittersweet.

Scene 25

Mary returns to the office and notices there is a board meeting on, which she wasn't told about; she is alarmed and looks slightly worried. She opens the door and finds Judith pitching Mary's presentation to the management team.

Judith: "…and that is how I feel we can really turn things around in the next fiscal year." (Sits down embarrassed at seeing Mary).

Mr Thomas: "Fantastic presentation Judith. Lots of insight into the next year. Well done."

Mary: "What is going on?"

Mr Thomas: "Mary, you've missed a brilliant presentation from Judith. (Condescending look) Pity your child's panto was today, perhaps Judith can give a recap to you later."

Mary: "But the board meeting was not until tomorrow."

Mr Thomas: "Judith asked for this meeting today as she was anxious to show us her presentation. Look Mary, there is no point being angry with Judith. You were the shooting star of this company. I really thought we would be following you into the future, but you've really let go these last few years. I'm not being heartless. I know why, but I have to put my company first. (Smarmy smile) I'm taking Judith for lunch. I think we've got our new board member here. I'm sorry, Mary."

Judith: (Sheepishly) "Of course…erm…Mary, I'd be happy to go over it." (Mr Thomas has walked to other meeting members and is out of ear shot).

Mary grabs Judith by the arm.

Mary: "That's MY presentation. I gave you that to look over and help me out and you STOLE it?"

Judith: "You shouldn't have been so scared of putting your ideas forward then."

Mary: "You waited till you knew I'd be away and called this meeting. You betrayed me, Judith."

Judith: "Tough. (Judith looks totally belligerent) Nothing you can do now; the promotion is mine, and you can't prove the presentation or the ideas are yours because you didn't have the confidence to tell anyone."

(Judith, looks triumphant)

Mary: (Behind clenched teeth) "Except you, you thieving bitch!"

(Judith just shrugs her shoulders as Mr Thomas takes Judith away to the smiles of the other board members).

Scene 26

Back at Mary's, she is making dinner as promised for God.

He and Gabby are at the table, while Mary is preparing food at oven.

Gabby: (Whispering to God) "I don't think she's in a good mood."

God: "I know, she's had a tough day at work."

Gabby: "What happened?"

God: "Oh, just someone let her down."

Gabby: "That's bad."

God: "Yes, very."

Mary: "Here you are you two." (Putting roast turkey down)

God: "Mary, I heard what happened today with Judith."

Mary: "Yeah."

God: "Surely you can speak to Mr Thomas and explain."

Mary: "Explain what? I have no proof that the presentation is mine. It will just look like jealousy, and me trying to get the promotion instead of her."

Gabby: "Mummy, don't be angry. It's Christmas anything is possible."

(Gabby smiles an innocent hopeful smile full of faith, unaware of her mother's disbelief)

Mary: "Yeah…another great result at Christmas time. Thank you, God! (Sarcastically raising her wine glass). Remember to eat your sprouts, honey."

Gabby and God look at each other and push them to the side of the plate.

Scene 27

It's the office Christmas party, everyone from the office is there.

Mary is standing alone; God is with Peter.

God: "Well Peter, this is your big night." (Nudges Peter)

Peter: "What do you mean, George?"

God: "You know. It's your chance to get close to Maggie… Christmas, dance, mistletoe…"

Peter: "Oh, I really don't think so."

God: "Well, let's just see. First of all, you don't really need them (takes off Peter's glasses) and bow ties are not cool (removes Peter's bow tie). Now why don't you go over there and talk to her?"

Peter: "But…"

God: "Go on!"

Peter walks towards Maggie who is chatting to some other girls, she notices Peter walking over and the conversation halts as she turns toward him slightly.

Maggie: "Hi Pete!"

Peter: "Hi Maggie."

Maggie: "You enjoying the party?"

Peter: "Yes, it's great."

Maggie: "You're not wearing your glasses?"

Peter: "No, gave them a rest tonight."

Maggie: "You look great."

Peter: "Really? Erm… thanks." (Snigger)

Just then Phil and Andy come over.

Phil: "Petesy! What you doing here? Don't you have some stamps to sort out?"

Andy: "Or some Star Trek comics to read." (Nudges Phil)

Maggie: "Why don't you two morons knock it off?"

Phil and Andy: "Ooooooohhhhh!"

Phil: "Pete's got a protector."

Peter: "Look, Maggie I'll see you later."

Maggie: "No, stay."

Peter: "No, it's fine."

Andy: "Aww, is Petesy in a huff." (Shoves Peter whose arm goes into the punch bowl knocking it over him. Peter slips and falls)

Maggie: "Peter!" (Goes to help him up)

Peter: "It's fine, just leave me." (He walks away)

God: (To Peter) "What are you doing? Get back there."

Peter: "Didn't you see what happened? I've made a fool of myself in front of her."

God: "No you haven't, get back over there and stand up to those idiots. Don't let people walk over you."

Peter: "It's easy for you to say, George. I just can't do it."

God: "Look over there. Those two idiots are hanging around her, if you want her, you need to fight for her. Nothing is easy, show her the man that you really are, find that inner strength that I know you have."

Peter: "Yeah…" (Peter is full of confidence and walks over to Andy and Phil)

Peter: "Leave Maggie alone."

Andy and Phil burst out laughing.

Andy: "And what are you gonna do pipsqueak!"

Peter: (Grabbing Andy's arm) "I said, leave her alone."

Andy takes a swing at Peter, he ducks and punches him, knocking him clear across the floor to the other side. Out cold.

Phil goes to punch Peter, he grabs Phil's fist and repeatedly punches him in the face with it, knocking him out.

Maggie: "Wow Pete, that was amazing!"

Peter: "Maggie, would you like to dance?"

Maggie: "I'd love to, but I can't really dance to this fast stuff."

God: "Leave that to me."

God jumps up on stage with band.

God: "Okay, for all you romantics out there, here is a classic for you."

God and the band start playing Nat King Cole's *L-O-V-E*, with God singing and sounding exactly like Nat King Cole. The band are stunned that they are playing it.

Maggie and Peter dance close, they kiss.

Peter: "So, can I call you Margaret now?"

Maggie: "No, Pete you can't."

Peter: "Oh, why not, I like the name Margaret."

Maggie: "That's nice but my names not Margaret, it's Magdalene."

Peter: "Oh right, (they both smile and keep dancing) I like that better."

Scene 28

It's later on at the party, God picks up two drink and goes over to Mary who is standing feeling solemn and isolated.

God: "Hi." (Hands her a drink)

Mary: "Hi, didn't know you could sing like that, you were amazing."

God: "Years of practice."

Mary: "You know, you seem to have a way about you that everyone loves."

God: "Well, I try, it's nice to be liked."

Mary: "No, it's something else. Getting the job here, the mugger, Gabby adoring you instantly. What is it about you?"

God: "What do you think? Don't you like me?"

Mary: "I do, that's what scares me. I hardly know you, yet I trust you completely. I just don't get it."

God: "Maybe you've had too much to drink."

Mary: "Hmph. I'm fine, I've not had enough; I mean what is it with Christmas anyway?"

God: "What do you mean?"

Mary: "I mean, it's meant to be a time of joy, and all it brings me is misery. Look at her (Looks at Judith, talking with Mr Thomas and other board members) all cosy, that should be MY promotion!"

God: "Oh, she'll get her comeuppance one day."

At that, the drink Judith is drinking turns to insects, she sees it, screams and throws it away, straight into Mr Thomas's face. Mary laughs.

God: "See, told you Mary, all you need a little faith."

Mary: "Ha! Faith in what? Christmas? God? There's no such being!"

God: "You mustn't say that."

Mary: "Why? Will he strike me down? Hmph. If there is a God, then he hates me."

God: "Of course he doesn't, Mary."

Mary: "Oh really? How do you know? Are you God?" (Laughs)

God: (pause, looks deeply at Mary) "Yes Mary, I am."

Mary: (Laughs a hollow laugh) "Good one."

God: "Mary, I'm not joking, I am God."

Mary: "What? George, you're not funny."

God: "I'm not being funny Mary, I AM GOD!"

Mary: (Mary glares at him, furious. She slaps him) "Just go, get away from me, get away, you are mad, how dare you play with me like that after I've confided in you, you are sick, that's what it is, you're sick, Go away!"

Scene 29

Mary storms out of the party to the balcony. God follows her.

God: "Mary, please believe me, I'm not lying."

Mary: "How could you? You think you're funny? You're sick."

God: "I'm telling the truth, I AM God."

Mary: "How dare you (slaps him again). I have opened my heart to you, and you mock me like this, just go away, I never want to lay eyes on you again?"

God: "Mary—"

Mary: (filled with hurt, betrayal and anger) "Go away, I never want to see you again."

God: "Mary, please—"

Mary: "ARE YOU NOT LISTENING TO ME? GO AWAY!"

God: "Mary, look down."

Mary: "What? (Feels strange and grabs God to steady her)

Mary looks down, they are both high above the city. Mary screams and grabs God.

Mary: "What the…?"

God: "It's okay Mary, you're perfectly safe."

Mary: (Mary looks stunned) "How can I be safe…I'm floating in mid-air! Are you really? No, this is not happening. This is a dream. I'm asleep!"

God: "No, you are wide awake."

Mary: (Her eyes widen) "Oh my God, oh my…you…you're really Him?"

God: "Yes, I am."

Mary: (Tears well up in her eyes, as she tried to comprehend it, then logic kicks in) "No wait, you did, you've tricked me, this can't be real. You put something in my drink. This isn't real."

God: "It is real Mary. Believe, just believe. I'm real."

Mary: (Realising the truth) "You're God… Oh no…I've slapped God!"

God: (Laughing) It's okay…though it's not the first time, Lucifer did have a go though."

Mary: "Why are you here?"

God: "I'm always here."

Mary: "No, I mean now why?"

God: "For you Mary. For you."

Mary: "But you hate me, don't (hesitates) don't you?"

God: "Oh Mary, of course I don't. How could I hate anyone?"

Mary: "But you took him from me."

God: "People die for so many reasons, but their rewards are infinite, and it may sound like a cliché, Mary, but everything really does happen for a purpose."

Mary: "What purpose? To break my heart?"

God: "What could I say that would change your mind? Some things are for the Almighty alone."

Mary: "What kind of an answer is that? Just take me down."

They float down to the balcony. Mary goes through. It is dark.

Mary: "Where is everyone? We've only been away a few minutes."

God: "Have we?"

Mary: "What has happened? Hello? Anyone here?"

Mary opens the door to her office and finds herself squinting at the bright sunlight, she is outside in a field full of the most beautiful and vivid flowers she has ever seen, it is almost dream like. Behind her, she sees fields of grass and hears the sound of children playing. There are figures in the distance, but they are blurred, and she can't see them properly.

Mary: "Where are we?"

God: "I think you know."

Mary: "Am I…have I died?"

God: "No, this is not your time."

Mary: "The children…?"

God: "Yes, I meant what I said, long ago. There will be no more tears, no more pain, just happiness. (Turns Mary around slightly) Mary, look ahead."

A blurred figure approaches, Mary can't make out who it is.

Suddenly the figure comes into focus in front of her; it is her husband, Joe.

Joe: "Hi Mary."

Mary: (Bursts into tears) "Joe!" (Grabs him).

Joe: "Hey baby, no tears."

Mary: "Joe, I've missed you so much."

Joe: "I know you have, but I've never left. You never leave the ones you love."

Mary: "But how do I go on? What about little Gabby, she is so young…" (Sobbing)

Joe: "You go on for me, for her and most of all, my darling, for you. You must live Mary and be happy."

Mary: "How can I?"

Joe: "Because I want you too and because you have a long life ahead of you and you must fill it with as much joy and happiness as you can for you, for Gabby and for me. (He tenderly brushes back a stray hair from Mary's face). Christmas is a time to celebrate, not regret. I want you to enjoy Christmas again, just like we used to. Honey, it would mean a lot to me."

Mary: "Okay, okay."

Joe: (Hugs her tightly) "Now you must go on, you must live."

Mary: "Please…don't go."

Joe: "Babe, I'll never go, please just be happy. Gabby needs a father and you need someone to care for you."

Mary: "How can I do that when I miss you so much?"

Joe: "You will, the right person will come, and love could be just around the corner (Gently puts his hands around Mary's face and moves in close to her). Promise me you'll start to live again."

Mary: "I promise."

They kiss.

Joe: "Goodbye gorgeous. (Looking to God) Thank you." (God nods and smiles)

Mary opens her eyes, she is back in the shop at the start of the story, holding the same work presents.

Shop assistant: "Madam? Madam?"

Mary: "Yes? What? Sorry."

Shop assistant: "Are you okay? I asked if you wanted them wrapped."

Mary: (Looks at presents) "What? No...no...I thought I was...can't remember...erm...these are no good. Sorry. (Dumps basket on counter). I'll get better ones than that. Sorry, so sorry."

Scene 30

Mary is leaving the store with loads of presents, she rushes out straight into a stranger, knocks him over, and the presents are scattered.

Mary: "Oh, I'm dreadfully sorry." (Goes to help him)

Stranger: "It's quite alright, here let me help you pick these up."

The stranger looks up as Mary helps him, he looks like God, though it isn't him. She smiles at him. She has no memory of meeting God, only that she is happy and more content.

Mary: "Oh, hi."

Stranger: "Hi."

Mary: "I'm Mary."

Stranger: "I'm George, nice to meet you Mary."

Mary: "Nice to meet you."

George: "Listen, I don't mean to be forward but would you like to grab a coffee?"

Mary: (Pause feeling confused and them smiles) "Yes, I would love to. Have we met before? (She puts her hand in her pocket and pulls out the USB stick with her presentation on it). I need to pop back to the office first, if that's okay? I need to show my boss something…"

They both walk away, chatting. Across the road, God is standing. No one can see him. He is smiling. A man approaches him.

Man: "Did you enjoy yourself?"

God: "Yes, I did."

Man: "Time to go back?"

God: "Yes, I guess. (Turns to look at Mary for one final time as she and George walk around the corner laughing, he

then turns to his companion) Oh, by the way,
...nday."

... "Thanks Dad."

...ey both walk away, God stops.

God: "Oh wait, I forgot something…"

Man: "What?"

God: "A promise I made… (looks up to the sky) now snow." (It begins to snow).

God lifts his face heavenward and smiles into the snow then turns to look at his companion.

God: "Okay, let's go home (Smiles)… Merry Christmas."

Man: "And God bless us, everyone."

The End